The White Indian Series
Book XXVII

CREEK THUNDER

Donald Clayton Porter

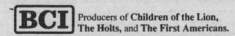

BCI Producers of **Children of the Lion,**
The Holts, and **The First Americans.**

Book Creations Inc., Canaan, NY • Lyle Kenyon Engel, Founder

BANTAM BOOKS
NEW YORK • TORONTO • LONDON • SYDNEY • AUCKLAND

45960564

CREEK THUNDER

A Bantam Book / published by arrangement with
Book Creations Inc.

Bantam edition / December 1995

Produced by Book Creations Inc.
Lyle Kenyon Engel, Founder

All rights reserved.
Copyright © 1995 by Book Creations Inc.
Cover art copyright © 1995 by Louis Glanzman.
No part of this book may be reproduced or transmitted in any form
or by any means, electronic or mechanical, including photocopying,
recording, or by any information storage and retrieval system,
without permission in writing from the publisher. For information
address: Bantam Books.

If you purchased this book without a cover you should be aware
that this book is stolen property. It was reported as "unsold and
destroyed" to the publisher and neither the author nor the
publisher has received any payment for this "stripped book."

ISBN 0-553-56143-X

Published simultaneously in the United States and Canada

Bantam Books are published by Bantam Books, a division of Bantam
Doubleday Dell Publishing Group, Inc. Its trademark, consisting of the
words "Bantam Books" and the portrayal of a rooster, is Registered in
U.S. Patent and Trademark Office and in other countries. Marca
Registrada. Bantam Books, 1540 Broadway, New York, New York
10036.

PRINTED IN THE UNITED STATES OF AMERICA

RAD   0 9 8 7 6 5 4 3 2 1

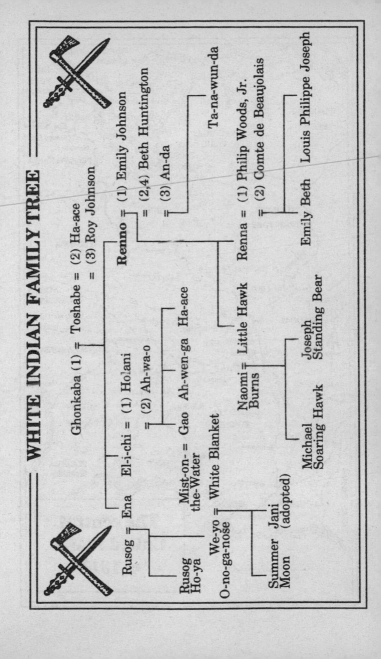

WHITE INDIAN FAMILY TREE

Ghonkaba (1) = Toshabe = (2) Ha-ace
= (3) Roy Johnson

Renno = (1) Emily Johnson
= (2,4) Beth Huntington
= (3) An-da

Ta-na-wun-da

Renna = (1) Philip Woods, Jr.
= (2) Comte de Beaujolais

Emily Beth   Louis Philippe Joseph

Rusog = Ena   El-i-chi = (1) Holani
= (2) Ah-wa-o

Mist-on- = Gao Ah-wen-ga Ha-ace
the-Water

Little Hawk

Naomi = Little Hawk
Burns

Joseph
Standing Bear

Rusog
Ho-ya

We-yo = White Blanket
O-no-ga-nose

Summer Jani
Moon (adopted)

Michael
Soaring Hawk

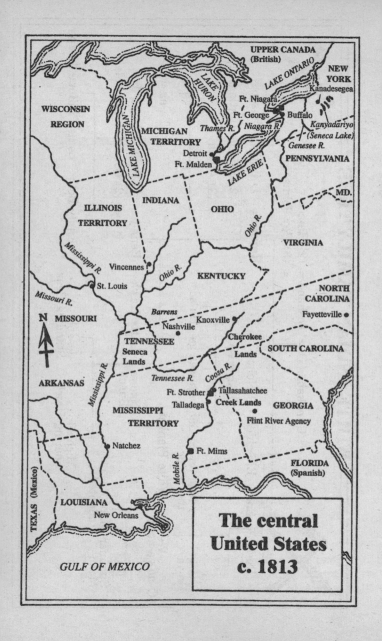

The central United States c. 1813

August 1813

"*My son!*"

Renno bolted upright in bed. He sat in the darkness, shaking his head.

"Are you all right?" his wife muttered, stirring beside him. When he did not reply, she touched his arm. "Renno, are you all right?"

"Yes, Beth. I'm fine." He patted her hand. "Just a dream."

"What about?"

"I . . . I don't remember."

"Lie down," she soothed. "Try to sleep."

He fell back against the pillows and lay staring into the blackness. His wife's breathing deepened, and when he was certain she was sleeping again, he rose and walked to the window.

Pulling the curtain aside, he stared into the night. Moonlight glinted across his broad, strong forehead, making his blond hair appear grayer than it was. At forty-nine, Renno was the fourth in a line of men known as the white Indian. His great-grandfather, for whom he was named, had been found as an infant by the sachem

Ghonka and raised as a Seneca. It was Renno's father, Ghonkaba, who had led some of their nation south to live with the Cherokee. Like his ancestors, Renno had been sachem of his people, but in recent years he had abdicated his position to his younger brother, the shaman El-i-chi. Still, Renno was given the honor and respect afforded a sachem.

This morning he did not feel like a sachem, for today he felt a strong measure of fear—something he invariably attributed to the white half of his blood.

It was only a dream, he told himself. Still, he could not shake the troubling images.

He understood that the best way to exorcise both the images and the fear was to confront them.

Alone. Like a sachem of the Seneca.

His feet and chest bare, Renno put on trousers and went outside, circled the house, and passed through the gardens. Leaping across a small creek, he started to run, guided by the pale light of the moon and his keen knowledge of the countryside. He entered the woods and quickened his speed until he was almost at a warrior's pace, his muscles tight with awareness as he raced along the path, dodging the trees that loomed up in front of him in the thin light.

The land gradually rose, and the trees grew sparser. Gaining the top of the ridge, he plunged down the other side into a broad, grassy meadow, then ran through another copse of trees and up a bluff that overlooked a broad stream. Here he came to a halt and stood with his hands on his hips, breathing hard, gazing across the valley to where the moon was settling into the west.

He knew that in the distance was the northward bend of the Tennessee River and beyond it the languid waters of the Mississippi. Farther still were lands seen only by their native tribes and by the few intrepid men who had dared the journey—among them his son Little Hawk, who had accompanied Meriwether Lewis and William Clark on their expedition to the Pacific Ocean.

Little Hawk was out there now, somewhere in the vast reaches of the Ozark Mountains of Missouri Territory. He was alone—and he was in trouble.

"Unless it was only a dream," Renno whispered.

But it had been a dream of such intensity that he could not shake the vision it had brought him:

Little Hawk writhing on the hard-packed earth. Clutching his side. Bleeding. . . . Three Creek warriors lying sprawled alongside him. Faces painted for war. Their eyes fixed in death. . . . A hand lifting Little Hawk's head. Caressing his long locks of yellow-gold hair. . . . A flash of steel. A whoop of victory. The scalping knife making its sharp, quick cut. . . .

Renno gasped and dropped to the ground. "No!" he blurted, pounding the earth, fighting the vision. "Not Little Hawk!"

"Who-o-o?" the wind seemed to call as it caressed his face and arms.

"I won't let you take Little Hawk!" he cried.

"No-o-o . . ." the wind replied.

Renno struggled to sit up, crossing his legs as he stared into the distance. Silently he called for them to come—the manitous of his ancestors.

They did not fail him. The first apparition was little old man. Indistinct, floating in front of him, it spoke in the Seneca tongue of Renno's father, Ghonkaba.

"No . . ." the manitou said, its voice one with the wind. "Little Hawk shall not die. The line of Renno and Ja-gonh and Ghonkaba shall continue."

"But the dream," Renno said, trying to focus on the face of the manitou, unable to see who it was. "What of the vision?"

"Do not be afraid. Os-sweh-ga-da-ah Ne-wa-ah"—it used Little Hawk's Seneca name—"walks the red path, though he does not see it. He will sit again at the council fire."

"But he has renounced the Seneca blood within him. He has turned his back on his ancestors."

"His ancestors do not turn their backs on him. And we will not turn our backs on Renno, son of Ghonkaba, grandson of Ja-gonh."

The manitou started to recede into the darkness.

"What must I do?" he called after it. "Why does this vision trouble my sleep?"

"Renno . . ." a soft voice, exceedingly sweet and familiar, whispered in reply.

"Emily!"

He struggled to see the face of his beloved first wife, but the moon had set, and all was darkness. Darkness and wind.

"Our son," the manitou said through the breeze. "Our son shall come home."

"Is he all right?" Renno asked. "Is he alive?"

"He shall come home. You shall see him again. Before you make the great journey."

"Is it me? Am I the one who will die?"

Something glimmered in front of him: hair as lustrous and golden as corn silk. "Be not concerned about the time or the place. You shall see your son again. You shall know who he is. The song shall be passed from father to son."

He sensed her withdrawing, and he reached toward her voice.

"That day, I shall be waiting," she promised, her voice caressing him as it faded into the night. "Then we shall journey beyond the river. Then I shall lead you home. . . ."

"Emily!" he called after her.

The wind echoed her name. And then she was gone.

Renno rose and took a step forward. To the west, the sky was pitch, but behind him he felt the stirrings of dawn. Turning, he faced the birthplace of the sun. It had not yet risen, but the blackness was giving way to streaks of blue. And low in the sky was a crimson glow, as if a council fire burned at the horizon.

"Home . . ." he breathed. "Little Hawk will come home."

Renno started down off the bluff. Heading east. Toward the sun.

Chapter One

 Hawk Harper hefted the long rifle once owned by his friend Meriwether Lewis. Lifting it to his shoulder, he sighted down the barrel and trained the gun at a point on the opposite side of the meadow. He held his breath, his finger tightening against the trigger.

Branches rustled, and the leaves parted at the precise spot he was aiming. Through the heavy mist he saw the animal emerge: a doe, almost as large as a buck. She hesitated, looking around the clearing, then took a few steps forward and nibbled at the grass.

Hawk chose a point on her midsection. As he pulled the trigger he saw a second animal, a young fawn, waddle into the meadow and stand behind its mother on gangly, unsteady legs. He tried to ease up on the trigger, but it was too late. The mechanism had already engaged, and the spring drove the hammer down onto the flashpan with a snapping *thunk*. The doe's ears rose. In the split second it took for the spark to ignite the powder and travel to the touchhole, Hawk threw the barrel skyward.

The explosion shattered the morning calm.

around, the doe leaped into the forest. The fawn hesitated, its body shaking with fear. And then it, too, was gone, racing into the underbrush after its mother.

Almost killed her, Hawk thought, shaking his head. Mother and child. Innocent. So close to death.

His eyes welled with tears as the memory took form. He saw the small body of his son Joseph Standing Bear sprawled lifeless on the ground, skull crushed, eyes plucked by vultures. He saw his wife, Naomi, lying dead beside the body of the Creek warrior Calling Owl, who had kidnapped and murdered her.

Mother and child.

They had died brutally, and brutal had been Hawk Harper's revenge. He had been known as Little Hawk then, but with their deaths he had disowned the one-quarter part of him that was Indian.

"Captain Hawk Harper," he whispered, trying to shut out the painful memories.

But he was not even Captain Harper any longer. He had resigned his Marine commission on the very eve of his appointment as President James Madison's military liaison officer. He had fully intended to report for duty after taking his surviving son, Michael Soaring Hawk, home to Huntington Castle. Months had passed since the deaths of his wife and son, and he had thought himself past mourning. But when the time came for him to set out for Washington, something had kept him from making the journey and had led him west instead, to live alone in these mountains and see if he could make some sense out of his great loss.

But he could not forget. He saw Naomi and Joseph each change of season, in every living thing. Nor could forgive, try as he might.

The weeks had become months. And still he did not hen he would be ready to return home, when he able to see his family and surviving son again.

Harper shivered and told himself it was from

the late-summer chill that had begun to settle each night over the Ozark Mountains. Leaning his rifle against a tree, he reached into the leather pack at his side for a sizable metal flask, uncorked it, and took a quick tug, feeling the warm whiskey burn the back of his throat. He started to replace the cork but raised the flask to his lips again and then again. Soon he was seated with his back against the trunk, his knees drawn up under his chin.

Hard drink did not agree with Hawk, but he no longer cared. He never bothered to shave anymore, and it had been more than a few weeks since he had last bathed in the creek near the cave that he called home.

"What does it matter?" he asked himself and took another gulp.

By the time he set out for home, his legs were as unsteady as that fawn's. He had managed with some effort to reload the rifle and hoist it over his shoulder, and now it balanced there precariously, the barrel swinging as he tottered along the narrow deer path. The forest grew quiet as he passed, birds and squirrels flitting for cover as if they knew the weapon might go off at any moment.

Usually Hawk moved silently through the woods—in the manner of the very ancestors he now rejected. This morning he didn't even try. Instead he burst into an old tavern song he had learned at West Point:

> "Bring 'round the whiskey, boys.
> Let all the maids be kissed.
> For when we march agin the king
> They surely shall be missed.
>
> "So raise high your flagons, lads,
> And to the maidens sing.
> For when the cocks have made their call
> We march agin the king."

Hawk downed the last of the whiskey and dropped the flask into his bag. It missed its mark and clattered to the ground, left forgotten alongside the trail.

He swung the rifle off his shoulder and clutched it against his chest. Throwing back his head, he laughed uproariously at some imagined fantasy, some remembered incident of his youth. His bellowing voice rose again:

> *"So raise high your flagons, lads,*
> *And to the maidens sing.*
> *For when the cocks have made their call*
> *We march agin the king!"*

The deer path widened, opening into a grassy clearing set against the base of a rocky escarpment. Stepping into the clearing, Hawk lowered the rifle butt to the ground and leaned against the barrel, steadying himself as his blurred vision adjusted to the glare of sunlight. With some effort, he focused on the jumble of rocks at the base of the escarpment and made out the entrance to the small cave he called home.

Assured that no one was about, he muttered, "All's well that ends well," then staggered across the clearing.

As he neared the cave a dark shape appeared among the boulders, and he stopped short, jerking up the barrel of his rifle.

What he thought might be a bear took human form as it stepped into the light: a man about thirty years old, wearing the distinctive paint of a Creek warrior. Two younger warriors came into view on either side of him, all three standing in front of the cave from which they had emerged—*his* cave.

Their appearance instantly cleared the fog from wk's mind. Gripping the rifle and swinging the barrel een them, he cursed himself for drinking too much naking such a commotion tramping through the He noted that the two younger ones carried firearms—old trading muskets from the looks of them—while their leader had only a bow and arrow. None of them were making any move to bring their weapons into play.

Warily, Hawk lowered the barrel but kept his finger on the trigger, reasoning that if he handled things right, there wouldn't be any need for gunplay. Raising his other hand, he called out, "Welcome."

The warriors looked at one another. Then the leader raised his hand and repeated the English greeting, followed by a few words in his language. Hawk shook his head, indicating he did not understand, though in truth he knew a little Creek—enough to be a better listener than talker. With the odds so much against him, it was far better to listen than to speak.

The man repeated his question in passable English, and Hawk replied, "My name is Harper. I am a hunter, and this is my home." He waved the barrel, indicating the entire clearing. "By what name are you called?"

"Thunder Arrow." The man pointed to his companions and introduced them as Running Fox and Talks-with-Clouds.

"You are welcome to my home," Hawk said, trying to sound as sincere as possible. He took a cautious step forward, then halted. When they made no hostile gestures, he moved closer and asked, "Have you traveled far?"

"Many days." Thunder Arrow signed that they were coming from the north.

"Then you must rest awhile from your journeying." Lowering his rifle all the way, Hawk gestured at the cave. "You may share my meal."

The young man named Running Fox whispered something to Thunder Arrow, his tone curt and somewhat agitated. From the few words Hawk picked up, he guessed the man was suggesting they kill him and take whatever he had. But Thunder Arrow cut him off with a sharp glance.

Turning back to Hawk, the Creek warrior nodded and said, "We share your fire."

They followed Hawk into the cave. It was not much more than a deep cleft in the escarpment, and quite a bit of light spilled through fissures in the rock above.

As the warriors sat around the fire pit, Hawk stood his rifle near the entrance but kept the pair of ornately carved pistols tucked under his belt. He gathered dry branches from a pile inside the cave and added them to the hot coals. When they crackled and burst into flames, he placed several small logs on top.

Hawk took out some dried venison and handed it to the three men. As he sat among them he noticed they were closely examining the cave, as if looking for something. He did not doubt they had already searched the premises. Nor did he doubt what it was they desired.

It took only a few minutes before Thunder Arrow came to the point with a single questioning word: "Rum?" He made a sign of drinking from a bottle.

Hawk weighed his options. It was likely they were making no moves against him because they had not found his stash of liquor. And they would certainly assume he kept such a stash, given his recent inebriated state. But if he shared his supply, they would have little reason to let him live. Then again, it was equally possible it would make them forget their natural animosity toward him. The one thing of which he was certain was that turning them down would be a sure route to disaster.

"Rum. Yes, let's have something to drink."

He could feel their eyes upon him as he rose and crossed to the cave entrance. Heading outside, he made his way among the boulders strewn along the base of the escarpment until he found the one marking where he had hidden many of his supplies. Moving some of the loose rocks, he retrieved a jug and carried it back.

They just want a drink, Hawk told himself as he reentered the cave. The three men were seated where he had left them, and indeed they did not appear threatening. They were Creeks, to be sure, and as such his sworn enemies. But those responsible for the deaths of his wife and son had already met their fate at his hand. There was no need for further bloodshed.

Let them have their drink. Then they will be on their way.

Removing the cork from the jug, he handed it to Thunder Arrow, who sniffed at it and nodded. Apparently he did not mind that it was whiskey instead of rum—if he even knew the difference.

The jug was passed eagerly from hand to hand. When it reached Talks-with-Clouds, who sat at Hawk's left, he took a long swig, then hesitated. Finally he grunted and thrust the jug at their host.

Hawk pretended to drink, then passed the whiskey back around.

"Where are you traveling?" he asked after the jug had made a third circuit.

Thunder Arrow said in the Creek tongue, "We are on our way home to Cusseta, in the south."

Hawk knew perfectly well what had been spoken. But guessing the man was testing his knowledge of their language, he shook his head and shrugged, indicating that he did not understand.

"We go home," the warrior said in English.

"Ah, yes. To your village?"

The man nodded. "Cusseta."

Hawk raised the jug. As the whiskey touched his closed lips, he jerked the jug away. *Cusseta.* The name came back to him in a flash—and with it bitter memories.

His eyes narrowed as he handed Thunder Arrow the jug. "Cusseta," he repeated, forcing calm into his voice. "Is that near the Flint River Agency?"

Thunder Arrow nodded and took a long pull at the jug.

Hawk felt his back stiffen. He had found the body of his beloved Naomi near Cusseta.

The jug continued its circuit, and Hawk could see

that the whiskey was having its effect. If he did not antagonize them and perhaps offered them a second jug for the trail, they likely would soon have their fill and be on their way. No need for bloodshed. No need for violence.

If he just did not push things.

Hawk passed the jug around yet another time, trying to remain silent, to let the matter rest. But then, before he realized what he had said, he had spoken the name aloud: "Calling Owl. Did you know Calling Owl?"

Thunder Arrow eyed him suspiciously. "You know of Calling Owl?"

"All of my people know the name Calling Owl."

Running Fox turned to Thunder Arrow and asked, "What does he say about Calling Owl?" Though he spoke in his own tongue and used Calling Owl's Creek name, he apparently understood what Hawk had been speaking about.

Paying no attention to his comrade, Thunder Arrow asked Hawk, "Why you speak of Calling Owl?"

Hawk shrugged as nonchalantly as possible. "Calling Owl was a great warrior. Yet we heard he was killed by a woman. Not just a woman but a white woman."

Talks-with-Clouds now pressed for an explanation of what was being discussed. Thunder Arrow turned to the warriors and said in Creek, "He has heard how Calling Owl was disgraced by that whore of a white devil."

Running Fox chuckled. "He took her like a dog, and she bit off his nose like a mountain lion."

"And cut off his manhood!" Talks-with-Clouds added, laughing loudly.

Thunder Arrow did not seem so amused. He looked back at Hawk and said in broken English, "You hear of Calling Owl so far away?"

Hawk's nod was solemn and threatening. "Calling Owl is known far and wide as a man who would spill the blood of a woman and child rather than face his enemy alone on the field of battle."

Thunder Arrow's hand eased toward the tomahawk

at his belt. Prodded by his comrades, he translated what had been said.

"Tell him how the white woman squealed like a pig as she died," Running Fox suggested, laughing even harder.

"And how our warriors first passed her around and tasted her pale flesh." Talks-with-Clouds snatched the jug from his friend's hand and took a generous gulp.

"Calling Owl was great warrior," Thunder Arrow said in English.

"He was a coward," Hawk Harper shot back. "A coward and a skunk."

Thunder Arrow stood, gripping the handle of his tomahawk. Hawk rose and faced him, his own hands not far from the pistols in his belt. Still seated, the other warriors stopped chuckling and stared up at the two men.

"Calling Owl was my friend," Thunder Arrow declared solemnly.

"As he was my enemy," Hawk replied. "Still, that is no reason for us to be enemies. Unless you would speak poorly of the woman he killed."

Sneering, Thunder Arrow spat out the words, "The white whore."

Hawk kept his tone calm and even. "That woman was my wife."

Thunder Arrow's eyes widened, and he whispered, "Little Hawk . . ."

His companions asked what had been said, but before the warrior could reply, Hawk turned to them and said in Creek, "My name is Hawk Harper, but Calling Owl knew me as Little Hawk. It was my wife who cut off his manhood and took from him the breath of the Master of Life. And it was my own hand that struck down his followers: New Man, Wild Wind, Eneah, Little Fox, Red Runner, and Gator Toe. Of those who were with Calling Owl when he kidnapped my wife, Stone Head alone still walks the earth. He lives only because I had had enough of killing."

Running Fox shot to his feet and exclaimed, "New Man was my cousin! You left him for the buzzards to devour!" He stood a bit unsteadily as he glowered at Hawk.

"What is in the past need not come between us," Hawk said in their tongue. "But you must not speak ill of the woman who was my wife."

Talks-with-Clouds rose also but with greater difficulty. His words slurred, he said, "Red Runner and Gator Toe were my friends."

"And the white woman was a whore!" Running Fox spat, drawing the knife from his belt.

Thunder Arrow alone remained calm. Letting go of his tomahawk, he raised his hand to restrain his companions. Fixing a cold eye on Hawk, he said in Creek, "You have shared your rum and your fire. We have no quarrel with you."

Turning, he motioned sharply for the others to leave the cave. Talks-with-Clouds complied, staggering out into the morning sun. Running Fox was more reluctant, but with a prod from his leader, he turned and stalked outside.

Thunder Arrow paused at the cave entrance. Looking back at Hawk Harper, he nodded and said in English, "Your wife brave woman. She honored your name."

Hawk returned the nod and stood motionless as the warrior disappeared into the glare of sunlight.

Realizing he was gripping the handles of his pistols, Hawk let go and rubbed his palms together. Walking to the cave entrance, he stepped into the light and watched the three men continue across the clearing. Running Fox and Talks-with-Clouds were talking to each other as they approached the trees. Thunder Arrow was farther behind and to their right.

As they gained the trees, Hawk started back into the cave. He was still turning when something slammed into his left side, followed by the sound of a gunshot. Thrown to the ground by the force of the slug, he spun around and caught sight of Running Fox at the edge of the trees, his musket smoking as he reloaded.

Even as Hawk jerked one of the pistols from his belt, he realized it was too long a shot. Dropping it, he crawled to his rifle, leaning against the entrance. He thumbed back the hammer and swung it around, praying the charge was still primed. Sighting down the barrel, he saw a puff of smoke from Running Fox's barrel, then heard the report a split second after the musket ball ricocheted off the rock wall beside Hawk's head.

Hawk held his breath and squeezed the trigger. The hammer snapped down, and there was a moment's hesitation as the spark set off the powder in the pan. Then the gun recoiled with an echoing boom, and Running Fox was thrown off his feet, the side of his face blown away.

As the acrid smoke cleared, Hawk spied Talks-with-Clouds racing toward him, musket at the ready. Close on his heels was Thunder Arrow, who looked as if he was trying to run down his companion.

Hawk drew the remaining pistol from his belt and in one smooth motion cocked, aimed, and squeezed the trigger. The hammer struck with a dull *thunk*. Thumbing it back, he pulled the trigger a second time, but the gun would not fire. Tossing it aside, he leaped for the pistol left lying by the entrance and heard the muffled boom of the musket and the whistle of the ball flying past his head.

Snatching up the pistol, he rolled and came up on his knees, firing at the warrior, now less than twenty yards away. But Talks-with-Clouds was prepared and dived to the ground as the gun fired. In horror, Hawk saw a spurt of red from the chest of Thunder Arrow, who was close behind. Thunder Arrow drew up short, staggered a few more steps, and fell to the ground.

Talks-with-Clouds was already on his feet. He sprinted the remaining yards between them, pulling a tomahawk from his belt as he came. With a terrifying yell he leaped at Hawk, raising the tomahawk above his head.

Hawk swung his pistol, slamming it into the man's hand as Talks-with-Clouds knocked him back into the cave. The young warrior managed to hold on to the weapon and viciously swept it down, just missing Hawk's head. Hawk smacked his pistol barrel into the man's cheek, knocking him to the side.

The two men went rolling. Talks-with-Clouds flailed away with the tomahawk, but Hawk managed to grab it and wrench it away. It spun through the air, landing at the edge of the fire pit.

The young warrior pulled himself free of Hawk and scrambled across the floor. His fingers were about to close around the tomahawk when Hawk landed on his back, shoving him aside. Talks-with-Clouds twisted around, throwing Hawk over him and onto the fire, but Hawk rolled clear. The warrior was instantly on him again, hands locked around his throat, thumbs pressing into his windpipe. Sputtering, Hawk tried to break the man's hold. But the grip tightened, and Hawk felt the heat of the flames only inches from his face.

Hawk's body went limp. His hands fell from the warrior's forearms to his sides.

Talks-with-Clouds continued to press, intent on choking the life out of his enemy. But his victim no longer struggled, and so he eased the pressure slightly.

Hawk struck with the speed of a snake. He drew the knife from his belt and drove it into the warrior's midsection, jerking it upward, through the stomach, the long blade piercing the heart. The Creek's body jerked; his nerveless fingers loosened, falling away.

There was a dull moan, then silence. Hawk rolled the body off and rose to his knees. Talks-with-Clouds's eyes were open, and for a moment Hawk thought he was making some sort of entreaty. Then the spirit passed from him, and his eyes glazed over.

Hawk pulled himself to his feet and thought he saw a shadow move out in the clearing. With that came the realization that one of the others might still be alive, and in a heartbeat he yanked the knife from the body at his feet and staggered toward the cave entrance.

He blinked, struggling to clear his vision as he came out into the glare of sunlight. Someone was kneeling at Thunder Arrow's side, but it was not Running Fox, whose body lay crumpled a dozen yards away. It was another warrior, and when he saw Hawk standing there, he jumped up and ran toward the forest.

Hawk cursed. The three men must have left a lookout in the woods—someone who might be on his way to summon other Creeks in the area. Forgetting his weakness and pain, Hawk took off at a run, his head still foggy and his vision a blur as he raced across the clearing and entered the woods only yards behind the warrior.

Branches slapped against his face as he closed in on his prey. He knew if he did not quickly overtake the Indian, his little remaining strength would be exhausted, and the man would get away. But he had the advantage of knowing these woods and was able to leap over fallen trees and other obstacles that slowed his quarry.

The underbrush thinned. He heard a cry and saw the shadowed figure only a few feet ahead. The fellow was shorter and slighter than his companions—possibly a young warrior on his first foray.

Hawk closed the distance between them, raising the knife in front of him. But when the man stumbled, Hawk barreled into him, the blade barely missing its mark as they tumbled to the ground. In an instant Hawk was up, spinning and lunging at the young warrior, who lay facedown a few feet away.

The Creek rolled over and gave a cry, hands raised to ward off the thrust of the knife, eyes open wide. Dark, frightened eyes—the eyes of a young woman.

Stabbing down with the knife, Hawk jerked his hand to the side at the last moment, and the blade sank into the soft earth beside the woman's head. She flailed at him, her fists smacking his shoulders and chest, her breath coming in ragged gasps that Hawk was surprised to find moved him. He managed to grab her wrists and pinned her to the ground.

"Stop!" he yelled, repeating it in the Creek tongue.

She stared up at him, her body rigid, her eyes filled with shock and fear.

"Don't move!" he ordered in Creek as he gingerly released first one hand, then the other.

She lay beneath him, her only movement the quick rise and fall of her chest and the darting of her eyes as she sought a path of escape.

Snatching the knife from the ground, Hawk held it in front of her as he rose to his feet. She wore the leggings and hunting shirt of a young warrior, but as he gazed down at her, he wondered how he had ever thought her a man. It did not surprise him that the three Creeks would not want such an attractive young woman to accompany them while they investigated the white man's cave.

Stepping back a few feet, Hawk tucked the knife under his belt. He felt strangely light-headed, and remembering the wound he had suffered, he ran his hand along his left side just under the armpit and felt the warm, sticky blood that was soaking through his buckskins.

"Get up," he told her, first in English and then Creek. He motioned with his hand, and at last she complied, standing up and brushing off her clothes. Finally he muttered, "Go on, get out of here," and gestured for her to leave.

She glanced toward the clearing where her friends lay dead and after a few moments of indecision set out in the opposite direction. When she hesitated again and looked over at Hawk, he waved her away, then turned his back on her and started toward the clearing.

Fog suddenly settled, closing around him. A cold, numbing fog. He shivered as he forced one leg in front of the other. His body was leaden, his head swirling like a leaf on a river.

He thought of his young son, his small skull crushed by Calling Owl's tomahawk. And of his wife's corn-silk hair matted with blood.

He had taken a musket ball, but he did not feel it. He did not even think about it. His mind's eye was focused on the faces of Joseph Standing Bear and Naomi. They called to him, and as his legs gave way beneath him, he went rushing toward their outstretched arms.

Chapter Two

 Ta-na-wun-da ran at a warrior's pace across the broad green meadow. Far to his right the waters of the Tennessee River glimmered a deep purple in the filtered afternoon light. Beyond it a bank of clouds eased across the grasslands, burnt-orange tendrils entwined around the sun.

The rifle tucked under his arm felt as heavy as a tree trunk, and he shifted it to his other side. His legs and lungs cried out for him to stop, to stand motionless in the middle of the field and embrace the final hours of what had been a perfect day. But he would not rest—not until he had crossed the ridge that loomed in the distance.

One more hill, he told himself. *Just one more.*

It felt good to be out on his own, running free, away from the Cherokee-Seneca village of Rusog's Town and the confines of Huntington Castle. Not that he spent all that much time at the home of his father, the sachem Renno. His father had seemed sullen and withdrawn this past year—ever since Ta-na's half brother, Little Hawk, had resigned his military commission and gone west into the Ozarks. Ever since Renno's eldest son. . . .

My son . . . he heard his father intoning. And Ta-na knew it was spoken for his brother.

"Little Hawk," he whispered between panting breaths.

In the months before departing, Little Hawk had stopped using that name, preferring to be called simply Hawk or even Harper, the family surname. And he had completely rejected his Seneca name, Os-sweh-ga-da-ah Ne-wa-ah, just as he had rejected his Indian blood.

The one-quarter part of him that is Indian, Ta-na-wun-da thought, shaking his head ruefully.

Ta-na, on the other hand, was three-quarters Seneca. He could not help but wonder if that was why his father did not seem to notice him.

"Little Hawk," he breathed. "Always Little Hawk."

Ta-na tried to shake loose the troubling thoughts. He was twenty years old—far too old for self-pity or regrets. If Renno favored his elder son over his younger, such was a father's right. Some would call it his duty. And Ta-na would do well to accept it as the will of the Master of Life.

If Little Hawk owned their father's heart, at least Ta-na possessed a full measure of the bloodline of the first white Indian, who had been named Renno like their father. In fact, Ta-na's grandmother, Toshabe, used to say that though Ta-na's hair and skin coloring had come from his full-blood Seneca mother, he had the features and physique of his great-grandfather, Ja-gonh, son of the first Renno.

Ta-na-wun-da shortened his stride but maintained his pace as he left the meadow and started up an incline toward the ridge. On the far side was a valley with a small stream running through it; he would rest there and take his evening meal. He might even make camp and return to Rusog's Town the next morning. He knew Renno would be annoyed if he stayed away the whole night—but his father would keep that anger to himself.

Not once during the past year had he questioned Ta-na's comings or goings. Not since Little Hawk went away.

Ta-na's own heart was heavy, though not from his brother's absence. True, he and Little Hawk had always gotten along well. But nine years separated them, and Ta-na had spent much of his childhood in the home of his uncle, El-i-chi. Though Little Hawk was his brother in the flesh, his cousin Gao, with whom he had been raised, was his brother in the spirit. In fact, he had suckled at the breast of his aunt, Ah-wa-o, alongside Gao, who was only a few months older.

Ta-na missed his cousin terribly, but more than distance had come between them. After marrying the young Potawatomi-French woman Mist-on-the-Water, Gao had joined the Pan-Indian movement led by Tecumseh, a prophet and war leader determined to drive the whites back across the great water of the Atlantic. To further those ends, Tecumseh had allied his forces with the British, who were battling the Americans in the frontier around Lake Erie. This placed Gao in opposition not only to the young nation but to his own family, who considered themselves Americans.

Ta-na had been thinking more and more about his friend in recent days. What had become of Gao? Was he well? Had he been injured in battle?

"He is fine," he declared, nodding. Of that he was certain, for they had been almost as close as twins, and Ta-na always felt Gao's suffering as if it were his own.

If something happened to him, I would know, he told himself.

Yet thoughts of his best friend were coming with marked frequency, leading Ta-na to suspect that something was about to happen—that some news of Gao's circumstances would reach him all the way here in the Cherokee Nation.

As Ta-na gained the ridge, he slowed his pace somewhat and sprinted down the slope toward the creek. A line of thin alders marked its banks, and he headed toward a broad bend where a calm pool had often provided him with fish. If he was lucky he would soon be roasting one over a campfire.

His luck held, and in less than an hour he had a low fire burning and several trout laid out on a hot stone. His pack contained a thin blanket, and he spread it in front of the fire and sat cross-legged upon it, stirring the coals with a stick.

Another hour passed. The sun was just touching the horizon when he heard people approaching from the south. Indians, he guessed from the sound of their moccasins.

Leaving the fire burning, he snatched his rifle and moved upstream, hiding in the underbrush from where he could see the campsite. A few minutes later the travelers emerged from the trees on the far side of the creek and waded across the water.

It appeared to be a Creek raiding party—an even half-dozen men, faces painted, muskets at the ready. They searched the campsite, emptying Ta-na's pack but making little effort to ferret him out.

Perhaps they will take what they want and leave, he told himself.

It would be readily apparent that this was the campsite of a lone person, and they might not waste time rousting him from his hiding place. Unless, of course, they were looking for a little entertainment.

Take what you want and go, he silently urged them. *Before it gets dark.*

But the sun had already dipped below the horizon, the light was growing thin, and they were making no effort to leave. In fact, three of them had seated themselves around the fire and were picking at the remaining scraps of trout. They appeared ready to settle in for the night, and they wouldn't want to leave a stranger—presumably armed—lurking somewhere among the trees. Ta-na was convinced they would soon search the area.

As he knelt in the bushes, rifle shouldered and

cocked, one of the men moved away from his companions and started toward him. The fellow was about Ta-na's age and size, his features obscured by paint, his head half hidden by a plait of feathers that cascaded down the left side of his face. He looked somewhat different from the others in both dress and physique, and for a moment Ta-na assumed he was their leader. But as he drew closer, Ta-na decided he must be from some allied tribe.

Even as Ta-na trained the rifle barrel on the stranger's chest, he knew resistance would be futile. His only hope was to make a run for it and pray they were poor shots. He would wait as long as possible; each second he delayed was another moment for the darkness to close in and assist his escape.

Stay calm, he told himself. *Let this fellow pass.*

But the warrior wasn't moving on. In fact, he seemed to possess an uncanny sense for where Ta-na was hiding. He walked to within a few yards of the bushes and stood gazing at them, trying to peer into their shadowed recesses. Beyond him, the Creek warriors began beating the underbrush closer to the campfire in an attempt to roust him out.

The Indian with the plait of feathers moved a few steps closer, held his palms forward as if to show he came in peace, and intoned, "Ta-na-wun-da."

An electric bolt shot up the young Seneca's spine. The voice was so familiar, yet almost unreal.

"Ta-na-wun-da," the warrior repeated.

Dropping his rifle, Ta-na leaped from the bushes and raced toward the man, arms wide in greeting as he shouted, "Gao! You've come home, Gao!"

As the cousins embraced, Gao's companions gathered around him, grinning and clapping him on the back.

Ta-na sat in front of the fire, listening as his cousin explained how he had been sent by Tecumseh on a mission to Creek country south of Tennessee. Gao and the Creeks had been on their way back north when he decided to visit his parents in Rusog's Town. Leaving his companions some distance from the village, he had gone in alone and spent a few hours—long enough to assure his family he was all right and to learn where Ta-na had gone.

"I still cannot believe you found me," Ta-na marveled when Gao finished his story.

"It really was quite easy," Gao professed. "When your father told me you were on a run, I knew I must either wait for you to return or go looking. My friends were eager to push on, so I decided to hunt you down. And where else would you be but along this trail, where we spent so many hours of our youth? When I saw this reckless fire, I knew it had to be my little cousin." He gave a teasing grin.

"This region has been at peace since Tecumseh went north," Ta-na replied, his look almost accusatory. "A man can make a fire without fear of losing his scalp." He gazed at Gao's companions, his jaw tightening.

Gao glanced over his shoulder at the Creeks, who were contentedly eating chunks of venison. "It's a good thing I am with them, cousin. If not, that beautiful long hair of yours might be gracing a Creek musket barrel."

"I suspect that without you, they never would have passed through Cherokee lands or Tennessee."

Gao nodded. "There is truth to what you say. The Creek have learned to avoid Andrew Jackson's country. When they must journey north, they travel on the far side of the Father of Waters." He used the Indian name for the Mississippi River.

Ta-na stared at his cousin for a long moment, then shook his head in amazement. "I would have loved to see your father's expression when you showed up in Rusog's Town."

Gao looked down at his outfit. "I was not dressed like this. And I did not have my Creek friends with me."

Ta-na chuckled. "I can only imagine what El-i-chi would have thought if you walked in like that." He leaned over and smudged his cousin's face paint with his thumb.

Gao slapped his hand away, then grinned sheepishly. "To be truthful, this was mostly for your benefit."

"You thought to put a scare in me, yes? And what if instead I had put a bullet in you?"

Gao chuckled. "Ah, so you learned to fire a rifle since I left." His eyes narrowed thoughtfully. "I knew you would do no such thing. Ta-na is far too cautious."

"You don't know that. Many moons have crossed the sky since we parted company."

"And in that time you have begun to soar free? Like a little hawk?"

Ta-na knew the comparison to his elder half-brother, in whose shadow he had always been, was intentional. He chose not to respond to the comment but instead declared, "I choose my own path."

"Then why are you still under the wings of our fathers? You can fly higher than a hawk. As high and swift as a ball of fire that streaks across the sky."

"You want me to fly on the tail of the Panther Passing Across," Ta-na said solemnly. He spoke of Tecumseh, who had been given the name Panther Passing Across because of the flaming ball of green fire that had lit the sky on the night of his birth.

"It is a good life in the Canadas. There we are not Seneca or Shawnee or Creek. We are one people, and we will have our land and our honor back." Gao leaned forward and grasped his cousin's forearm. "Come with me, Ta-na. It is our destiny."

Ta-na frowned but did not pull his arm away. "Is it our destiny to be slaves to the British? Since when have they cared what becomes of us? Their coats may be red, but their skin is as white as the Americans they fight."

"The British are less than nothing," Gao spat, sneering with contempt.

"Yet you fight at their side."

"Their guns will help us drive the Americans from

our land. And when that is finished, we shall send the redcoats scurrying back to their ships."

"No, Gao, you will not. The British lost this land; they will not reclaim it. The only thing Tecumseh's war will accomplish is to harden the hearts of the Americans against all of our people."

"Their hearts are already hard." Gao smacked fist against palm.

"You speak of my father's people."

"Renno is a sachem of the Seneca. His blood may be mixed, but his spirit is red."

"And what of my blood . . . and yours? Do we not have a portion white?"

"The red has long since drowned out the white," Gao declared.

"And you would have me drown the oath my family has taken to the Americans?"

"The Americans do not keep the many promises they have made to our people," Gao argued.

"We are speaking of *my* word—no one else's. Would you also have me turn against my father? And what of your father? Does El-i-chi's heart not ache to see you join arms with Tecumseh?"

Gao's gaze lowered, and he shook his head. "We did not speak of Tecumseh. He saw from my eyes that my path was set. He did not try to talk me from it."

"Then do not try to talk me from mine."

Gao looked up, his eyes entreating. "Is it truly your path, Ta-na? Are you certain this is so?"

Ta-na hesitated. "I know only this: It is not my path to take up arms against the people of my father and my grandfather and his father before him."

"Are you so sure?"

He folded his arms over his chest. "If such is my path, let the manitous tell me it is so."

"So now Ta-na-wun-da speaks to the manitous?"

Ta-na allowed himself a small grin. "I have always

spoken to the manitous. They just do not choose to reply."

Gao smiled as well. "Nor to me. That is why I put
my faith in a prophet with a human voice."

"I am pleased for you, Gao. Pleased that you are so
certain of your path."

The two men fell silent. When at last they spoke
again it was of more pleasant topics. Ta-na described the
things he had done during the past year—and the young
Cherokee and Seneca women he had wooed. Gao told of
his life with Mist-on-the-Water and how his heart ached
for her while he was gone.

It grew late, and they settled in for the night. As
they spread their blankets and prepared to sleep, Gao
made one final entreaty.

"Ta-na-wun-da, in the morning I return to where
Tecumseh is gathering warriors in the north. I want us to
part as brothers and friends, so when the sun rises I will
trouble you no more about this matter. But tonight I
must ask one last time if you will reconsider and take the
red path. If it is your family that concerns you, know that
Tecumseh assures us that when the Americans begin to
retreat, our families and our people will see that this is
the will of the Master of Life. They will know that Tecumseh speaks the truth, as he did when he warned that
the earth would shake."

Gao referred to the great New Madrid earthquake of
January 1812, an event foretold by Tecumseh as a sign for
the Indian nations to unite against the white invaders.

"When they see the truth of the Panther's words,"
he continued, "then we shall walk the red path together."

"I am already upon that path," Ta-na declared. "But
it does not lead me to the north or to Tecumseh."

"Then I shall wait until our paths meet. And I shall
pray that the Master of Life brings that day soon." Gao
rolled over and pulled the blanket around him. "Good
night, Ta-na-wun-da."

"Good night, my cousin . . . my friend."

* * *

The next day, Ta-na-wun-da walked briskly up the broad, straight lane that led to Huntington Castle, the home of his father, Renno, and stepmother, Beth Huntington Harper. The lane, just outside Rusog's Town in the Cherokee Nation, was lined with pecan trees, with split-rail fences enclosing the surrounding pastureland. The white clapboard house at the end of the lane was more correctly called a mansion. Since there were no brick-making kilns in the Cherokee Nation, it had been constructed of native timber and sported a pillared front veranda. Craftsmen hired in Knoxville and Nashville had done the interior work, and furnishings had been brought from as far away as England to fill the twenty spacious rooms.

Ta-na halted at the end of the lane. He had only been away for a day, yet now as he looked up at the building, gleaming white in the early afternoon sun, he realized how out of place it was here in Cherokee country. Somehow that seemed appropriate, for the owner was not Cherokee but half Seneca and half white. Like this house, Renno did not always look as if he fit into his surroundings. Yet he moved effortlessly between the dual worlds of his ancestors.

Things were not so clear-cut for Renno's younger son. He often wore white men's clothing, although it made him feel ill at ease. Yet Ta-na was sometimes accused of not thinking like an Indian, and he had to admit there were moments when he simply did not know what to think.

He stared down at his buckskins—not Seneca or Cherokee or even white. Then he gazed back up at his father's home and shook his head ruefully. Truly he did not belong here in Huntington Castle. But where was his home? In what world did he fit?

"Ta-na!" a voice shouted, and he turned to see his father rounding the corner of the house. "You are home!"

The young man felt awkward and self-conscious as

Renno hurried over and clasped his forearms. Ta-na covered his feelings by asking, "Did you see Gao?"

Renno's smile faded. "He was here yesterday. I fear he has broken his father's heart."

"Gao must walk his own path."

"That boy had better come to his senses. Anyone who believes Tecumseh can overcome the westward march of white settlers is a fool. Their numbers are too great . . . like the stars in the night sky."

"I think in his heart Gao knows this to be so."

"Then why does he fight alongside Tecumseh? To take up arms against the United States is to die. It is that simple."

"There are those who would rather die free than live as slaves."

"Are we slaves?" Renno asked, waving a hand to indicate their home and the land surrounding it.

"I fear the day will come when even this will be taken from our people," Ta-na replied. "We will be forced to walk a bitter trail beyond the Father of Waters to an unknown home and an uncertain future . . . whether we are full-blooded or only one half."

"Were you off on a run or a vision quest?" Renno asked, his tone tinged with scorn. When Ta-na did not reply, he took a step back and looked his son up and down. "Or perhaps it was your cousin who put such dark visions in your head. Did he convince you to take up arms against your own people?"

Ta-na hesitated a long moment before finally shaking his head. "I do not choose Gao's path of blood. But I understand it. And I suppose a part of me even envies it."

"Things are not as simple as Tecumseh would have us believe. He would defeat the Americans by siding with the British. Even should he succeed, it would not reduce the number of whites any more than my plucking a single strand of hair would make me bald. It would only place a less sympathetic ruler in Washington."

Ta-na sighed. "I know that you speak the truth. But still my heart is troubled."

Renno came up beside Ta-na and wrapped an arm around his shoulder. "I know just the thing for a troubled heart. One of Beth's hot meals."

"Yes. I'd like that."

"Then we will speak no more of Tecumseh. And if we mention Gao, it will be to wonder how he is handling that young wife of his. From what he told us, she is quite a beauty."

"A spirited one," Ta-na added, remembering the last time he had seen her at Vincennes.

Renno led his son toward the veranda. "And what of Ta-na-wun-da? Is there a spirited beauty in his future?"

Ta-na grinned. "Many. There will be many."

Chapter Three

 Hawk Harper lay on his side and gazed down a long, dark tunnel toward a distant point of light. It drew closer, larger, blazing and dancing with all-consuming radiance.

Such is death, he thought and felt strangely at peace.

A figure moved in the light and stood haloed by it. A manitou of his father's people? he wondered. An angel of his mother's? A friend?

Naomi . . . he breathed, his voice no more than a faint rush of wind.

The face of the angel was shrouded in darkness, so great was the flaming halo of light at her back. But he saw her long, flowing hair and imagined it as golden as the sun. He gazed upon her lush, graceful figure and knew that soon he would be in her arms.

Naomi! he called again as he tried to reach out to her. He wanted to run to her, hold her close, breathe the aroma of her, and know that he was home. At last.

But he could not move—could not even raise his arms. And with a shock of fear he knew he would have to leave her again. It was not yet time.

And with that thought his beloved turned away from him. She turned to face the light.

"No!" Hawk shouted, railing against the angels, the manitous, the Maker of Life. Raging against God.

He felt heat at his back, as if another light was ablaze close behind him, drawing him back. Away from Naomi, away from God.

"No! No! No!" he screamed, struggling to hold on to her, afraid to let her go.

She heard his desperate cry, for she turned toward him again. She moved away from the light and came closer, down the long tunnel, until she was hovering in front of him, kneeling at his side.

"Naomi!" he cried, his eyes flooding with tears as he tried to make out her features through the shadows.

"Shh . . ." she whispered, placing a hand on his lips. Then she spoke something in a language he did not understand.

The language of the angels? he wondered.

The light flickered at Hawk's back. It danced across her face: skin soft and coppery, features delicate yet sharp, long hair that gleamed like a raven's wing.

She spoke again, and now he recognized the language as she told him, "Lie still."

It was the language of the Creek.

Hawk lay there, afraid to speak, unable to move. The young Creek woman rose and moved passed him. He heard her stirring the embers of a fire and felt its heat as it flared up behind him. As it cast a warm, shimmering glow on the walls of the cave.

The woman returned to his side and knelt in front of him, her touch gentle but her expression exceedingly sad, almost lifeless. She said, "Do not move," then stood again and started back down the tunnel through which she had come—the tunnel formed by the cave entrance.

Outside, the great light continued to rage. She walked to it, then disappeared off to the side. When she came back into view, she was dragging something along the ground. Hawk watched as she hoisted it with great effort and dropped it onto the blazing light.

It was indeed the light of death. It was a funeral pyre, and she stood framed by its glow as it consumed the bodies of her Creek companions.

"My brother . . ." Ma-ton-ga whispered, gazing up as streamers of smoke curled into the blackness above. "Be on your way, Thunder Arrow. May Running Fox and Talks-with-Clouds walk always at your side."

The pyre flared brighter, branches crackling with heat, hair and flesh and sinew hissing as they singed and charred. When she could bear the sound and smell no longer, Ma-ton-ga backed toward the cave. Turning, she ducked through the entrance and approached the white man. The one who had killed her brother.

He was in the other world again, eyes closed, breath shallow, completely unaware of her presence.

It is better this way, she told herself. She would not have to imagine him looking at her. She would not have to wonder what he was thinking or see the image of her brother reflected in those terribly cold, terribly blue eyes.

She had observed enough from the shelter of the forest to know that this white man had not drawn the first blood. Before the gunfire had erupted, she had thrilled to see her brother and his companions leaving the cave and coming to where they had left her. She had told them that they did not need anything the white man had to offer. They only needed to be on their way to the Creek lands in the south.

But Running Fox had been greedy. No sooner had they entered the woods than he had called out that he would not let the white man live another day. Then his musket had spoken, and it was answered by gunshots from the cave. And soon they all were lying dead: Running Fox, Talks-with-Clouds, and her beloved Thunder

Arrow. All but the white man, who hovered between the worlds of shadow and light.

He must be a great warrior among his people, to best three Creek warriors, she mused as she stared down at him. But a great man did not hide himself away in a hole in the mountainside. Perhaps he had the yellow-metal fever, though there were no signs that he had been digging in the earth or fishing rocks from streambeds.

He must suffer from the firewater madness, she told herself. Had they not heard him singing like a crazy one when he first appeared?

The young woman knelt beside the unconscious man and touched a lock of his hair. Never had she seen hair so golden or a face so strong and mysterious. It was true that he had the pale skin of his people, but it had been bronzed and toughened by the sun until it was almost as richly colored as her own. There was something familiar about him—something she could not identify. It was as if a part of him had come from the same source as her people.

Ma-ton-ga slowly drew forth the knife, which she had painstakingly cleaned and oiled after removing it from the white man's belt. She ran her thumb sideways across the blade. It was the sharpest edge she had ever felt; it could sever a man's throat as easily as a blade of grass.

She leaned over and held the knife close to his neck, watching the reflected firelight dance along his skin. She thought of how it had sliced open Talks-with-Clouds, spilling his blood upon the ground. She thought of the blood of her brother and Running Fox soaking into the earth.

Ma-ton-ga gently pressed the blade against the white man's throat. As her pressure increased, a trickle of blood oozed up along the edge of the metal. The man stirred but did not awaken, his head turning slightly, away from the knife.

"Thunder Arrow," she breathed. "Guide my hand. Steady my arm."

Again she placed the blade against his throat. She imagined his blood running free, his body being torn by vultures or joining her brother upon the pyre.

She wanted to cry, but she had forgotten how. Thunder Arrow was dead. And with him had gone all her feelings, all her tears.

She drew the knife upward under his chin, then along his cheek. Long, steady strokes, taking care not to break the skin as she scraped away the heavy stubble of beard, exposing the smooth flesh underneath.

She worked slowly and meticulously until his beard was gone. Then she stood and gazed down at her handiwork. Shaking her head, she circled the cave and rummaged in her leather travel pack for a strip of beaded cloth. She returned to where the man was lying and tied it around his head, smoothing his hair into place.

Clean shaven and wearing a woven headband, he looked like the warriors of her tribe. A warrior with sun-bronzed skin and long, golden hair. A white Indian.

Hawk Harper parted his lips, felt the steam of the dandelion broth as the Creek woman spooned it into his mouth. He tried to swallow, gagged some of it back up, then managed to down a mouthful. When she tried to press the spoon back between his lips, he turned his head to the side. Even that small movement sent a wave of dizziness through him.

He had lost a lot of blood, but he would live. He was not certain such a prospect pleased him.

"What . . . what is your name?" he muttered in her language, glancing up at her.

It was not the first time he had asked, and again she did not reply. Instead she rose, crossed to the fire, and poured the broth back into the iron kettle.

When she looked back at him, he thumped his chest and said, "Hawk. Hawk Harper."

Seeming totally disinterested, she turned away and busied herself tending the fire.

The routine was the same since he had regained consciousness the night before. She would prepare broth and feed him, taking almost no nourishment herself. Then she would dress his wound and tend to any other chores—including emptying and cleaning the small pot in which he was forced to relieve himself. Hawk, in turn, would try without success to get the woman to speak. What little communication she offered was in the form of signs, though he knew she understood what he was saying. The only information he had managed to pry out of her was he had been unconscious for a day and a half.

"Enough of this," he told himself, jerking aside the blanket that covered him.

With a supreme effort of will, he pulled himself to a sitting position, then pushed up onto his knees. By the time the woman saw what he was doing, he had managed to get up off the floor and was standing on extremely wobbly legs, clutching his side.

"No!" she cried out in English as she rushed over to him.

"So you *do* speak," he exclaimed, his grimace giving way to a smile.

She tugged his arm to make him lie back down. When he did not cooperate, she turned her attention to the bandage—a poultice of crushed and boiled herbs held in place by a strip of cloth tied around his chest. Satisfied the wound had not opened, she frowned at him and walked outside. When she returned, she handed him a long stick, gesturing that he should steady himself with it. Then she went back about her business.

Hawk's first foray from the cave was only a few steps into the clearing—far enough to see that she had cleaned up all signs of the pyre. Then he hobbled back in and tried to sit down. He almost fell over, and the woman had to come over and grip his arm as he lowered himself onto the blanket.

At the end of the day, the woman slept on the far side of the fire. In truth, she hardly slept at all, for every time Hawk glanced over at her, he saw her looking back at him. Her expression was hard to decipher. He could see she was concerned about his health, much as a doctor might be for a patient. But there was something else—a mixture of anger and fear. It made him wonder why she had stayed and helped him. He had taken the lives of her companions; the spirits would not have blamed her if she had left him lying where he fell.

Every now and then he saw something in her eyes that suggested a more sinister motive—that she worked so hard to heal him so he would be fully conscious when she exacted revenge.

Hawk shook off the thought. It was a preposterous notion, and he was ashamed it had even occurred to him.

The next two days passed in much the same fashion: The Creek woman took care of the chores, while Hawk Harper grew steadily stronger. Soon he was able to tend the fire and cook his own meals. He no longer had to use the makeshift chamber pot and was even able to wash in the small stream at one end of the clearing.

Just before dawn five days after he was shot, Hawk was awakened by the Creek woman poking at his arm. She had already built up the cooking fire, and the walls of the cave seemed to dance in its glow. As his eyes adjusted to the light, he realized she had prodded him with the barrel of one of the Indian muskets.

For an instant he thought his time of reckoning had come. But then she raised the barrel and slung the weapon across her back, tightening the beaded strap so that it would not slip off her shoulder. Reaching down, she placed Hawk's knife on the ground beside him. Then she circled the fire and hoisted a leather pack over her other shoulder.

Picking up his knife, Hawk tossed aside his blanket

and stood. He watched her walk toward the cave entrance and tried to think of something appropriate to say.

"Thank you," he called, following her outside. He repeated the words in Creek.

She turned to him and nodded, then started across the clearing.

"Wait!" He moved toward her as quickly as he could manage.

She waited but kept her eyes lowered.

"I . . . I am sorry," he said in her language when he stood in front of her. "I did not want it to end that way."

She nodded but still did not look up.

"I want you to have this." He held out his knife. When she shook her head, he said, "It is yours."

He reached for her hand and placed the knife handle in her palm. Her fingers closed around it, and she gazed at it a long moment. Finally she looked up at him. There were tears in her eyes.

"Thunder Arrow was my brother," she said in Creek.

"I am sorry. Truly I am."

"Yes. I know."

She tucked the knife beneath her belt and started to walk away. But then she hesitated. Turning back around, she clapped her hand against her chest and intoned, "Ma-ton-ga."

Hawk smiled. "Thank you, Ma-ton-ga."

She returned his smile. Then she continued across the clearing and disappeared into the forest.

"Ma-ton-ga," he whispered after she was gone. Then he repeated her name in English: "Place-Where-the-Sun-Sleeps."

He thought of his beloved Naomi. She and little Joseph had gone ahead to that place where the sun sleeps, leaving him alone in this land beneath the sky. Though he wanted to follow, he was not brave enough for such a path. Instead of defending himself against Ma-ton-ga's warriors, he could have accepted their bullets and tomahawks as a fulfillment, a grace. Instead of struggling against death, he could have taken that final journey.

Was it Ma-ton-ga who had saved him? he wondered. Or was he simply too much of a coward to die?

A warm breeze poured from the cave at Hawk's back. He could almost see it as it swirled around him and followed Ma-ton-ga's path into the woods.

"You are the breath of the Master of Life," Hawk whispered. "Carry away my anger and pain. And carry my love to that place where the sun sleeps. To Naomi."